To my parents, Doreen and Patrick Gilbert,
for all their love and encouragement
A. Y. G.

Text copyright © Sophie Piper
Illustrations copyright © Anne Yvonne Gilbert

Original edition published in English under the title "*Jesus is Born*" by
Lion Hudson plc, Oxford, England. Copyright © 2016 Lion Hudson

First Good Books edition, 2016

Good Books books may be purchased in bulk at special discounts for sales
promotion, corporate gifts, fund-raising, or educational purposes. Special
editions can also be created to specifications. For details, contact the
Special Sales Department, Good Books, 307 West 36th Street, 11th Floor,
New York, NY 10018 or info@skyhorsepublishing.com.

Good Books is an imprint of Skyhorse Publishing, Inc.®, a Delaware
corporation.

Visit our website at www.goodbooks.com.

10 9 8 7 6 5 4 3 2 1

Library of Congress Cataloging-in-Publication Data is available on file.

Cover design by Lion Hudson plc
Cover illustration credit Anne Yvonne Gilbert

Print ISBN: 978-1-68099-187-1

Printed in Malaysia

Jesus Is Born

Retold by Sophie Piper

Illustrated by Anne Yvonne Gilbert

Good Books®

The story of the first Christmas has been told and retold for some 2,000 years. From the Gospel of Luke, in the Bible, we know this story:

In the little town of Nazareth, in Galilee, lived a young woman named Mary. She had promised to marry a man named Joseph, and the wedding was not far off.

Then, God sent the angel Gabriel with a message for her. Mary gasped in fear at the sight of the heavenly being.

"Don't be afraid," said the angel. "God has chosen you to be the mother of his Son. You will name him 'Jesus.' He will bring God's blessing to the world."

Mary was astonished. "That can't be true!" she replied. "I can't be a mother before I'm even married."

"With God, all things are possible," replied the angel.

Mary bowed her head. "I will do as God wants," she replied.

It was not long after that another messenger came to Nazareth. This second one was sent by the Roman emperor who ruled the land.

"Everyone must go to their hometown," he declared. "They must enter their names on a list of taxpayers. The emperor demands taxes from everyone."

It so happened that Joseph's hometown was Bethlehem. "We will go there together," he told his bride-to-be. "For you and the baby you are expecting will be my new family."

Of course, there were many people going to Bethlehem for the same reason as Joseph. When he and Mary reached the town, there was no room left in the inn.

The couple had to shelter in a stable. There, where a donkey shuffled and an ox slowly munched, Mary's child, God's only Son, was born.

On the hills nearby, some shepherds were out watching their sheep through the dark and danger of the night.

Suddenly, an angel appeared.

"I bring good news!" cried the brightly shining figure. "Tonight, in Bethlehem, a child has been born: God's chosen king.

"He is the one who will rescue you from all your woes!

"He is the one who will bring God's blessing to the world.

"Yet, tonight the newborn sleeps in Bethlehem,
wrapped in swaddling clothes,
cradled in a manger."

Then the sky was filled
with angels, all singing,
"Glory to God in heaven;
On Earth, peace."

All at once the sky went dark.
The shepherds were astonished.
Had they all been dreaming?
Or had they really seen
angels, and was the message true?
     They hurried off to the
darkened streets of Bethlehem.

But where should they look?

A glimmer of light led them to a tiny
room where they found Joseph and Mary
and the baby, just as the angel had said.

Mary's eyes sparkled with joy as
they told their news.

Not many miles away, in the city of Jerusalem, another story was about to unfold: a story we know from the Gospel of Matthew, in the Bible.

In the royal palace there lived a man named Herod, who ruled the surrounding land on behalf of the Roman emperor. He had heard troubling news. Strangers had come to the city from lands to the east, and they said they were looking for a newborn king.

"We study the night sky for signs," they explained. "When we saw a new star, we believed it was a sign that a king had been born to your people, the Jews."

Herod was not a godly man, but he knew the stories at the heart of the Jewish faith: that one day God would send a king as great as their greatest king of days gone by—a king like David. He wanted no such rival to his power!

Accordingly, he summoned the chief priests. "This ancient promise of God sending a king," he said, "remind me what the stories tell us: where will he be born?"

"In Bethlehem," replied the priests, "the very place where King David was born."

Herod smiled grimly as he made a secret plan.

"If any child is being set up as a rival king, I will get rid of him," he said. "I'll send those strangers to find out who it is."

As those same strangers were directed to the Bethlehem road, the new star shone on their way. It led them to the hilltop town and the very house where Mary was, with her son, Jesus.

They brought out their tribute gifts:
gold, frankincense,
and myrrh.

That night, in a dream, an angel spoke to them.
"Do not go back to King Herod. He means
to harm the child."
They returned to their home country
by a different route.

In a dream, an angel also spoke to Joseph.

"Beware: King Herod will soon send soldiers to Bethlehem to kill any child who might grow up to believe himself king.

"Get up now, while it is night, and take Mary and Jesus to faraway Egypt.

"For Mary's child, Jesus, is God's own Son; and you must keep him safe.

"When he grows up, he will bring God's blessing to the world."